FROM ERIK'S DIARY
(LORELAI AND I)

EPISODES 1 and 2

DECEPTIVE DECEPTION

AN INTRIGUING GUEST

I0533103

Massimo Indrio

© Massimo Indrio
www.massimoindrio.com
first edition: November 2014
ISBN: 978-88-940304-1-9
Translation by Brett Auerbach-Lynn

EPISODE 1

DECEPTIVE DECEPTION

CHAPTER 1

The sky was red as fire and the clouds were traveling at the speed of light. I went to the window and pulled back the curtains. Looking out over the gray, peaked roofs of the houses, I thought, "Let's hope what happened the other day doesn't happen again, when that refrigerator fell out of the skyscraper onto that taxi."

Lorelai was cooking three eggs with salted tomatoes and singing that same tune she'd been mewing the day I found her under Giunfruss Bridge several months before – an evening when it had rained with the fury of ten tropical hurricanes put together.

What was it that had struck me about her? Maybe it was the depth of her eyes, that pale blue-green color you find only in people from the southern part of Northern Europe; or maybe it was the fact that she was fluent in sixteen sub-Saharan languages, dialects, and tongues.

"I was an idiot to have brought her here," I thought. "Surely nothing good can come of this. What a fool I've been. I truly am crazy. A madman, a nutcase, a lunatic! I've totally lost it! I'd kick myself - if only I could!"

Lorelai's lipstick-colored mouth chirped from under the vaporous cloud of her blond hair, "The eggs are ready, sweetie pie!"

How many times had I told her not to call me that, especially when we had company over! However, at the moment it was just us, so there was nothing I could do but sit at the table and choke down those damned over-cooked eggs, with the help of a couple of glasses of unripe cucumber juice, the beverage of choice of almost everyone who stopped for more than three months in Riversmill, that notorious border city on the border of a borderless territory bordering on a borderland.

And yet, just the same, I had to tell her. The moment had come. I had put it off, put it off, put it off, but now I felt I could put it off no longer. How it irked me to have to tell her! I struggled to swallow the hardboiled ostrich egg the girl had prepared for me. The more I chewed, the pastier my mouth felt; the pastier my mouth felt, the more I chewed. Chewing on glue would have been more pleasant. If I had chewed on a tire cover, I would have been happier. But would I have truly been happier? This I would never know, short of having a nice chew on a tire cover. Suddenly a bolt of lightning came in through the window, crossed the entire room, passed through the entranceway, and went down the stairs. But I was so immersed in my thoughts that I hardly noticed. Lorelai was slightly more aware of it since it had drawn a nice divider through the middle of her hair, blackening it just a bit.

"Listen, dear," I said to her. "You know that Lieutenant Bolfon from Homicide turned up a worn-through woman's boot in the river last night ..."

"Finish your eggs," she interrupted me, smiling with that smile of hers, somewhere between ironic and sardonic, that had always made me furious.

"Damn the eggs!" I shouted as I threw the remnants of the ostrich eggs at her.

Lorelai managed to dodge them by a whisker.

"I'm sorry, Lorelai," I rushed to apologize as I took my head in my hands in an attempt to unscrew it. "I don't know what I'm doing anymore, but you know how things have been lately, what with taxes ... the measles ... the antenna ... the battleship ..."

"What battleship?" she asked, stupefied.

"That's what I wanted to talk to you about, but I didn't have the courage."

"Tell me about it, please tell me about it. You should know you can tell me anything that comes into the anteroom of that brain of yours, even the most abstruse, absurd, extravagant, and astonishing things. In fact, these happen to be my favorites."

"Yesterday I was at an auction," I said, "and I purchased a battleship."

"A battleship? A battleship? A battleship?!" yelled Lorelai, beside herself to the point that she had risen to her feet and was throwing her hands wildly into the air. "Have you gone crazy? Just where are we going to put a battleship? In the garden? We don't even have a garden! Have you by chance forgotten we don't have a garden? When have we ever had a garden? A garden? A garden? This is just great! What's gotten into you! Pff! Shh! Huhh! Ahhh!"

CHAPTER 2

I got up from the table and sunk into the orange leather couch, the one near the plastic bear, and lit up a guncotton cigar that immediately started spraying its usual irritating sparks.

"Forget about the garden for a minute and calm down," I said, my stare piercing through the wall in front of me with the ease of a knife through melted butter. "I knew you wouldn't understand anyhow. Now please, bring me the pudding."

"The pudding? What pudding?" Lorelai snapped, her eyes scrunching.

"Today is Sunday, so I thought there was pudding."

"Pudding? Just where is this pudding story coming from? And today isn't even Sunday."

In truth it was Sunday, but where Lorelai was from they stuck Sunday in between Tuesday and Wednesday, so I thought it was better not to insist and changed the subject: "A battleship, don't you get it? Do you even know what a battleship is?"

"Don't worry, my wacky little sweetie pie," said Lorelai, as she sat on my knees scratching herself like a flea-infested kitten. "We'll just stick it under the bed." I looked at her seriously; then said, "I really think it's better we call Sergei Mussovrinski."

"Sure," said Lorelai with the expression typical of a boiled sole in a blond wig, "when you don't know what fish to fry, you always call Sergei Mussovrinski."

"So what, do you have a better idea?"

"Yeah, let's go to the town fair."

Ignoring her, I picked up the phone and started to dial the number, but after the first thirteen digits, the doorbell began to ring. I had never heard it ring quite this way. It was a sad yet at the same time disquieting tune that made me fear the worst.

Lorelai ran to open the door with speed of a gazelle on roller skates, but when she did so, she must have wished she had never gotten up. She could have continued reading some stupid fashion magazine or sipping on a shake, some tea or some coffee. She jumped up and screamed. It was him, all right: Sergei Mussovrinski. He hadn't changed a bit since the last time we'd seen each other at the lizard races, except that this time he had a kitchen knife planted in his back, a fork stuck in his chest, and was completely enclosed by a single, huge, parallelepiped of ice.

As Lorelai raced around the table screaming

and simultaneously cleared off the dirty dishes left from dinner, a series of questions spontaneously popped into my mind: just how had Sergei Mussovrinski come to be there? How had he managed to ring the doorbell? Who would now pay back the ten dollars he owed me? Why was chocolate pudding, when I ate it in the evening, so hard to digest?

I found a wheelbarrow and brought him inside. Damn, this was all we needed. Now the day was completely ruined. What had come over Sergei to do such a thing to me? I'd just recently closed my detective agency and wanted to start selling fruit tarts over the Internet, and now here I was again, back on the dance floor. And the trouble is - I'd never liked dancing. Lorelai, on the other hand, couldn't get enough of it, and would have danced even if she'd been locked in the broom closet with a bucket over her head. She didn't need music, either: she was practically always dancing, continually, even when she wasn't. I'm not sure if I've made my point.

I turned on the fireplace and placed Sergei Mussovrinski in a tub before it. Meanwhile Lorelai had calmed down and returned to her usual carefree self. But when the doorbell rang a second time, it was really too much for her and she ran to hide under the bed. Just so there were no misunderstandings, before opening the door I grabbed my reliable Fergusson K-16 double-barreled oblong carbon-reinforced pistol from it case. I opened the door to find the postman, or so he seemed - but I wasn't about to let anyone off quite that easily, so I pointed the gun at him and told him to come inside. He mumbled something about needing my signature, but I was wise to his game and tried to get the upper hand. It wasn't going to be easy to make a fool out of me, especially not on this rotten April day during a long winter in which everything seemed to be spinning out of my control. I was wide-awake, attentive and vigilant, like an owl suffering from insomnia. I caught a fly on the fly but, after a brief trial, I had to release it for lack of evidence. After tying the postman to a chair with a cord taken from the heavy velvet curtain that separated the living room from the kitchen, I grabbed him by the collar and shook him repeatedly, asking him without any useless formalities, "Why did you kill Sergei Mussovrinski?"

He remained silent, but I let him know right away he wouldn't get very far with that strategy.

Lorelai appeared, having emerged only slightly dusty from underneath the bed, and when she saw the postman tied up like a sausage, she got between us, shouting: "No, not him! It can't have been him. I know him too well!"

Everyone froze for a moment, and then I hissed at her, "Oh yeah? And just how well do you know him?"

She immediately caught herself: "Who me? I've never seen him before. I don't know any postman named Jonathan."

"So your name is Jonathan, is it?" I asked the sausage tied up like a postman.

"So what, you have a problem with that?" he exclaimed, freeing himself from his bonds with an expert Ju-fritzu move. Then he pulled a machine-gun out of his pants and began shooting around like a lunatic: left and right, in front and in back, above and below, as if he were surrounded by packs of bloodthirsty coyotes, vultures and moles.

A bullet grazed Lorelai's ear and knocked off a Max Petalòn earing which had cost me an arm and a leg.

I lost control. The blood went straight to my head, I was blinded with rage and for the usual three minutes I turned into the hairy, sharp-toothed monster Grunz.

Jonathan the postman froze with fear, and I took advantage to disarm him, carry him down to the cellar and chain him inside the family crypt, where the eleven rebel kings of the ancient kingdom of Strunzenhain are buried.

CHAPTER 3

By the time I got back upstairs, I'd turned back into my normal self but I was still afraid of Lorelai's reaction. Instead, her behavior was completely different from what I'd expected. She threw her arms around my neck, chirping, "My handsome beast! Why didn't you ever tell me you knew how to transform into Ambrose the wolf?"

I later found out that Ambrose the wolf was her favorite character in a story her grandmother used to tell her, trying unsuccessfully to frighten her.

But I was in no mood to whisper sweet nothings; so I coolly told her I had things to do, climbed up to the library in the tower, and immersed myself in the study of any cased I could get my hands on that had anything to do with freezing. As I always did after turning into the monster Grunz, I had a terrible headache; though, by now, I had learned that the pain could be alleviated if I simply banged my head repeatedly against the wall.

After hours of careful study, I had something

of an idea, but as often it happens in such cases, it was a decidedly bizarre idea.

Suddenly, I heard Lorelai's voice calling me. For crying out loud! Since that woman had come into my life, it was simply no longer possible to find a few hours of peace and quiet to explore the abyss of my own stupidity! I came down to find her waiting for me at the bottom of the stairs. She seemed agitated, like that time we had had guests over and she had burned the onion omelet.

"What's wrong?" I asked her, trying to disguise both my aggravation and my developing cold.

"Hurry, sweetie pie, hurry!" she cried, taking me by the hand and pulling me with her. "Come see what happened!"

When we reached the fireplace, I couldn't help but be shocked. The tub where I'd left Sergei Mussovrinski to defrost was filled to the brim with water, but there wasn't a trace of Mussovrinski! This was unacceptable! Where the hell had Sergei Mussovrinski gotten to now? There were only nine possibilities: 1) someone had entered silently and removed the cadaver; 2) once Sergei had completely defrosted, he had regained his senses and walked out; 3) Lorelai had a split personality and had hidden, or worse, devoured the cadaver; 4) a bridge in the space-time continuum had opened up and Sergei had ended up in some damned parallel dimension; 5) the killer was

Professor Van Strakken, who had discovered a way to freeze bodies such that they dissolved upon defrosting; 6) the tub was actually the cauldron of some crazy medieval wizard; 7) both Lorelai and I had fallen victim to a shared hallucination; 8) we'd been hypnotized by some ridiculous charlatan hypnotist; or finally 9) Betty the maid had come and, motivated by her obsession for order and cleanliness, had thrown everything out in the dumpster down in the alley. Knowing her, it wouldn't have been surprising. But at the moment, the most plausible hypothesis seemed to be the fifth, the one regarding Professor Van Strakken, the mad scientist. First of all, he hated Sergei Mussovrinski ever since the latter had had him arrested for that story of the French fries; and secondly, the diabolical scientist had just gotten out of prison after thirty-five interminable years in that Cayenne pit-of-hell. I imagined that he hadn't passed a single day without dwelling his terrible plans for revenge. Yes, all things considered, Professor Rudy Vladimir Von Strakken had a million reasons to hate Sergei Mussovrinski. But what he hadn't considered was that in order to kill Sergei and get away with it, he would have to get rid of me as well, for I knew the whole sordid story. But were we really sure that he hadn't considered it? A chill ran down my spine and a cold sweat broke out on my forehead. My stomach snapped shut, my hair stood on end and my knees buckled, while my teeth locked and my feet froze. This lasted no more than half an hour, however, for my steely constitution immediately put me back in control of my nerves, the clouds disappeared from the sky, and it was clear to me what my first move had to be. I took Lorelai and locked myself in the bedroom with her for a couple of hours.

CHAPTER 4

Afterwards, while we were having tea in front of the infamous fireplace and tub, I suddenly remembered Jonathan the postman, still down in the crypt. Perhaps he had now been softened up and would be ready to talk. I took a flashlight and rushed down the stairs, but when I reached him, things were not as I'd expected. Instead of having softened up, Jonathan the postman was now stonier than a marble statue, and he greeted me with a mocking laugh and words that cut like knives: "So you've come back after all, you turkey!"

"Turkey?" Nothing could have been more unexpected than to be called a turkey. When we were kids, my brother Fred used to call me a turkey from time to time, but that was another story.

I pretended not to have heard and asked him: "So, have you got your tongue untied?"

"What do you want from me?"

"Does the name Von Strakken mean anything to you?"

"You mean the mad scientist who was imprisoned for thirty-five years in Cayenne?"

"Yeah, that's him."

"Or do you mean the Von Strakken who sells watermelons on Donkey Square?"

"No, no. That first one."

"Which one was that?"

"The mad scientist."

"Him I don't know. Never heard of him."

I realized I would never get anything out of him if I didn't change my tactics. I decided to adopt the method of the carrot and the stick.

"Would you like to get out of this damp crypt?"

"No."

"What would you say to a Ferrari?"

"No."

"A villa on the Côte d'Azur?"

"No."

"How about spending the night with the most beautiful woman in the world?"

"No."

I had to admit that, sometimes, the carrot-and-stick method simply doesn't work, so I grabbed him by the collar and yelled in his face, "What do you want in return for talking?"

"I challenge you, turkey - ah ah ah! A duel, down by the river. You choose the weapon. If you win, I'll tell you what you want to know, and if I win you let me go."

I've never been able to turn down a challenge, so I accepted, though Lorelai begged me to change my mind and come back to bed with her. While this certainly was tempting, I stood firm in my decision. I believe that once you've come to a decision, you've come to a decision. If you order a pizza with capers, you can't later say that you wanted it with mushrooms.

Thus, the following morning at dawn we went down to the river as agreed. The cries of the seagulls cut through the fog which, not yet having had either the time or the means to dissipate, lingered nearby doing what it does best: enveloping things and obscuring their shapes. Wrapped up in my finest black cloak, I was strangely calm. Lorelai hadn't wanted to come because, as she said, she couldn't bear violence. In truth, there were also several other things she couldn't bear, such as opera and films about pirates.

The weapon I had chosen for the duel was the *kriss*, that famous Malaysian dagger with the sinuous blade, which I'd then dipped in the poison *karkàk*, a hallucinogenic psycho-stimulator. I'd added this last touch because I was certain of winning. Indeed, I had hoped this potent drug would help loosen the tongue of that tight-lipped postman. I unchained him and then presented the red, velvet-lined case containing the poisoned daggers, so that he might choose his weapon. The treacherous letter-carrier chose his weapon all right, but then, while I was trying to free my thumb which had become stuck in the case's zipper, the coward stabbed me in the left arm, producing a wound that would have been of no consequence had the blade not been poisoned. It goes without saying that I immediately regretted having dipped the daggers in *karkàk*, but now it was too late. My head began to spin and everything around me suddenly went black. Then a blinding light flashed before my eyes, or maybe inside my brain, and for a brief moment I had a vision of my wet nurse chasing after me with a soup ladle. Then I felt something in my stomach, as if I were being punched repeatedly, and finally I received various revelations regarding the future of humanity, up to the point where I lost consciousness and fell into the river.

CHAPTER 5

I'm not sure how long I was out cold: hours, days, months … Then, little by little, the fog in my brain began to disperse and my memories started to resurface. I remembered that damned Jonathan the postman, Sergei Mussovrinski, the blond Lorelai, the battleship, the whiskey with cherry juice, the ice cube pierced by an arrow, and everything else. When I finally opened my eyes, I realized that the reality of the situation was far from rosy - I was lying on a piece of wood that in the best of times must have been the door to some lurid cantina, but which now could do no better than float around like some stupid inflatable mattress smack in the middle of the ocean. I realized, however, that I ought to be grateful to that miserable raft, battered, and yet still strong enough to support me, since it had prevented me from playing a relaxing game of chess with good old Neptune, a few dozen meters below my current position.

While I was no stranger to uncomfortable situations, I'd never been a damned castaway adrift on the ocean with no chance of survival.

On the fifteenth day without food or water I was beginning to get a little antsy, when I saw a point on the horizon that didn't appear to be one of the usual whales sauntering back and forth across the ocean. This was definitely something different, and the closer it came the less it resembled a whale, and the more it resembled that which every respectable castaway hopes to see on the horizon.

I was already preparing to rejoin the world when the unexpected hit me, a cold shower on my hopes. The trouble is that sometimes you expect a caress, you close your eyes, you lean forward smiling, and instead you receive a nice punch on the nose. So when the men on that ship hoisted me on board, the first thing I asked them, after taking a quick look around me, was neither water, nor food, but rather that they put me right back on my raft and forget as quickly as possible that we had ever met. If ever there'd been a gang of pirates with the worst kind of criminal faces, well, these were even worse. The scum of the scum of the scum, if you catch my drift. Terrible, scarred and twisted faces, charred by the sun, hacked-up, ugly, disheveled, with expressions so ruthless they would have scared off the most ferocious guard dog and sent him running back behind the dresser with his tail between his legs. Such were the faces glaring at me, like a lion glaring at a gazelle that's mistakenly appeared on his doorstep. But I didn't lose heart, telling them, "Enough stories and joking around: either you give me a cabin with a porthole or the deal's off."

Some people simply have no sense of humor and are incapable of grasping irony. Or perhaps the real problem was one of language, my language to be precise, of which those illiterates seemed to have no knowledge whatsoever.

They began to talk among themselves more and more excitedly. If only Lorelai, with all the languages she knew, were here with me now! I couldn't understand their words but from their gestures I grasped that some wanted to cut my throat, some to turn me into cannon fodder, others to keep me as a slave, and still others to throw me back into the sea. I naturally sided with this last group. Refusing to leave my destiny to the whims of a pack of brutes, I interrupted their discussion and got so worked up, even if I could hardly understand anything, that with a shove I put the one who appeared to be their leader on his back. For a moment, everyone froze. I saw forty or so expressions of fury converge on me. But their leader was on the ground, moaning and complaining, like a millipede whose shoes are too tight. I immediately realized the cause of his whimpering: a huge splinter had gotten stuck in his hallux - that being the big toe on his foot. This was my chance. I threw myself on top of him and extracted it. A toothless smile lit up that brute's horrible face and, from that moment, my situation changed radically. There was an infinite series of handshakes, incomprehensible compliments, pats on the back and the like, after which a banquet was laid out in my honor. This was the menu: appetizer: canned tuna; first course: canned tuna; second course: canned tuna; fruit: canned tuna; for dessert: canned tuna. Apart from the lack of variety on offer, there was also something strange about the taste of that tuna, so I glanced at one of those little cans, only to discover it had expired in 1974.

After vomiting three of four times I began to feel a bit better, and little by little my anger towards those wretches gave way to commiseration. Poor guys! Piracy was clearly no way to make a decent living. I wished I could do something to help them, but I was already in enough trouble myself.

I had them let me off the ship at the nearest port, which happened to be in eastern Russia. When I arrived in the main square, there were few people around and it was freezing cold. I was alone, far from home and I missed Lorelai, and moreover, I was wondering just where Jonathan the postman, whom I had to thank for all this, had holed up. I raised my fist to the sky and shouted to the wind: "I'll get you one day, damned postman!"

A whip whistled through the air and wrapped around my wrist. I turned around and … I could not believe my eyes. There was no doubt about it, even if he was wearing a fur busby, a long, fur-lined coat and had grown a beard - it was him all right: Sergei Mussovrinski, alive and well as a hog in a mudbath.

CHAPTER 6

With a quick move, I freed myself from the grasp of his whip and walked toward him, smiling with arms outstretched.

"You old goat," I said to him, "I thought you were dead and gone! You'll have to explain this whole story to me, and just how you got here!"

Winding up his whip, he replied, "Sorry, I take wrong person. I think you be Ivan Popoff."

"Ivan Popoff, what!" I yelled, outraged. "Do you expect me to believe that you're not Sergei Mussovrinski?"

"My name Boris Voralexejeff. You take wrong person too."

I grabbed him by the collar, shook him and yelled in his face, "Sergei Mussovrinski, do you take me for a fool?"

The man whistled so shrilly that my ears were cleared of all their wax, and immediately there arrived next to him a large Siberian wolf, growling and glaring at me with that same fierce expression I'd seen from the pirates.

"Okay, I get it. You're not Sergei Mussovrinski," I said. "But you sure bear a striking resemblance." I decided to play along, but several questions continued to buzz around in my head. Who was that man who claimed his name was Boris? What did I really know about him? Who were his parents? Did he have brothers, sisters, grandparents, aunts and uncles? What was his shoe size? Had he had his flu vaccine? Did he like oysters? But above all, how could it be that he looked so much like Sergei Mussovrinski? We went to drink a dozen or so glasses of vodka in a tavern as filthy as a pigsty, but warm enough to unfreeze the blood in our veins, and thus we became quite friendly. I discovered he spoke my language, though not very well, as he had worked for several months – wouldn't you know it! – in the very café beneath my house. He also knew Lorelai very well, or so he told me. I was plagued by a doubt, the usual one - just how well did he know Lorelai? But this was no time to get into an argument, for in the meantime my ebullient mind had already come up with a plan, and that man was part of it.

I offered him money to come back with me to Riversmill, and I only had to negotiate for an hour and a half before he accepted. The problem now was how to get to the airport, since it was five-hundred kilometers away and these were five-hundred kilometers of arid, ice- and snow-covered steppe, given that it was the middle of winter. We opted to rent a sled, but when Boris' Siberian wolf realized we were counting on him to pull it, he categorically refused. We tried everything to convince him, but to no avail. I had a few other ideas on how to get to the airport, but when I shared them with Boris he found them laughable. The following evening we were back in the tavern, drowning our disappointing lack of progress in vodka, when we overheard a conversation at the next table. We discovered that the daughter of a Russian billionaire, a certain Tatiana, was passing through town and looking for both a bodyguard and a pilot for her biplane: destination Mountainsmill, only fifteen miles from Riversmill!

Even though I know I shouldn't, sometimes I act impulsively. I got up, grabbed the guy at the next table by the collar, shook him, and asked, almost yelling, just where the devil this Tatiana was. Taken by surprise, he told me but then he thought about it and threw a punch I was able to dodge. A huge brawl ensued in which nearly all those present participated. More than just fists were flying: bottles, glasses, seats, tables, shoes, hats, hardboiled eggs, cats and dogs. Though it was quite entertaining, after a while Boris and I snuck away and went to the Golden Ruble Hotel where Tatiana was staying. I immediately noticed a beautiful, red-haired girl with sunglasses sitting in the hotel lobby and thought it must be her. I approached and whispered in her ear, "Tatiana?"

Less than moment later I found myself tied to a chair in the hotel cellar, surrounded by about fifteen ugly mugs, one of whom was intent on torturing me with his Malay boot. The fact was I'd guessed wrong. That red-headed broad wasn't Tatiana the billionaire's daughter, but Svetlana, the daughter of the hotel owner who was a boss in the Russian mafia. And these guys, the gangsters, had thought I was a killer sent by one of their innumerable enemies to kidnap her or worse. I was already more than a little agitated because of the damned chain of events that had brought me here, such that it only took two or three turns of the Malay boot to turn me back into the hairy and sharp-toothed monster Grunz. I thought I was dealing with a pack of hardened criminals used to committing the worst possible crimes. I was mistaken. They ran away like chickens and left me alone with my rage, which I then vented against the Malay boot, remodeling it into a statue of Eros and Daphne that would not have looked bad at all in the living room, on the little table, next to the blue-checkered couch.

CHAPTER 7

When I returned to the hotel lobby, I found Boris in friendly conversation with the real Tatiana, a small, slightly plump girl with green hair and purple lipstick, a rather questionable color combination. I discovered that while I had been down in the cellar with the gangsters, Boris had succeeded in getting us hired by the billionaire's daughter – me, him and his wolf from the Russian steppe. I asked him why he'd neglected to come down and give me a hand, and he told me he had yet to finish weighing the pros and cons of such an intervention. This didn't seem like much of answer to me and I'd have liked to give him a piece of my mind, but the usual headache following my transformation into the monster Grunz was splitting my head in two, so I went to bang my head against the nearest column until the pain subsided. I then asked Boris how much this dame was going to pay for our services. He told me a hundred bucks a head, but then I saw him receive a briefcase from her out of which, after opening it in secret, he extracted a one-hundred-dollar bill for me. I didn't know if I could trust him, but I was in no rush to insult him either, as I wasn't exactly in cordial relations with his Siberian wolf. In any case there was no time to lose, because Tatiana had expressed the desire to get moving right away, and in fact her bags were already packed. There were four of them, and since it was up to Boris and me to carry them, we had to take two each. And I'll be damned if those weren't the heaviest bags I had ever lifted in my life. I imagined that perhaps Tatiana's father was in the construction business and she was bringing him a new shipment of bricks.

Anyway, apart from her strange taste in colors and her awful habit of lugging around suitcases full of bricks, the girl was all right. She was always telling jokes, and even if they didn't all make you die of laughter, at least one out of every five or six was pretty decent, and Boris thought so too. The Siberian wolf, however, was less appreciative of her sense of humor, though at times I thought I saw the beginnings of a smile; but it might have been he was just growling. It is quite likely that, on the freezing Siberian steppe, their sense of humor tended to be on the cooler side.

Tatiana's biplane was not exactly around the corner, and when we finally reached it my arms felt as if they had been lengthened by about ten centimeters. Boris, on the other hand, seemed much fresher and more relaxed, and I began to suspect that he had stuck me with the heavier bags. After loading them all into the trunk, I thought I might lift up one of the ones he'd carried to see if my doubts were justified, but a growl from behind me made me think twice. The conviction that I had found in Boris a faithful and loyal companion in arms, however, was beginning to waver. It was now time to depart, at any rate, and we all climbed aboard.

While the young heiress was perched on a fuchsia-colored armchair (a color she'd clearly chosen herself) in the passenger area, Boris and I withdrew to consult.

Initially, however, our conversation struggled to get off the ground - I looked at him, he looked at me, and then we both looked down at the ground or out the window.

Finally it was he who broke the ice, saying: "So, now we leave."

"Okay" I replied. "Raise the anchor."

"I agree."

"We certainly don't want to keep our dear Tatiana waiting."

"Certainly not," he agreed.

"The weather looks good."

"Let's hope it not rain later."

All this dillydallying could only mean one thing- neither of us knew how to fly the damned airplane. But the music had already begun and I was not about to back out now. Without another word, I spun around and headed into the cockpit. Perhaps Boris felt relieved by my resolution, though there was no point in hoping he would show it, as he wasn't one for emotional displays. He had the impassible face of an experienced poker player, or maybe that expression had frozen on his face as he was crossing the frigid Siberian steppe. As I sat down in the pilot's seat and fastened my seatbelt, I thought, "Surely it can't be any more difficult than driving a car!" So I turned the key and switched on the engine. For a beginner, my take-off wasn't half bad, apart from the little trim we gave to the highest branches of a row of trees that had foolishly gone and crowded around the end of the runway. The trouble began immediately after- I wasn't able to stabilize the plane which seemed as if it had a bad case of the fidgets. It was going up and down, left and right, and at times it jerked like a frisky horse. Rather than being on an airplane, it seemed as though we were on a ship in the middle of a tempest. The passengers who had unwisely neglected to fasten their seatbelts were thrown around in all directions. I heard moans and screams coming from the cabin, but no one came up to the cockpit to protest, perhaps because they were unable to make it that far. When, after the first three hundred kilometers, I finally managed to keep the plane more or less horizontal, I saw Boris sit down beside me, a bit disheveled but still impassive.

I said nothing at first, and then I asked him:

"How's Tatiana?"

"She jump with parachute half-hour ago. Before jump, she say: 'Have stomach in ears.'"

I decided not to comment and we continued flying like this, in silence, for another good hour.

CHAPTER 8

I had learned pretty quickly how all those buttons, levers, and cursors worked. The only one I had yet to try out was a black button which both intrigued and intimidated me at the same time, possibly because of the skull and crossbones it displayed. Though the temptation was strong, I decided to pass and concentrated instead on the question that was monopolizing my attention at the moment, that being just where in hell were we going?

The problem was that night had fallen as suddenly as a hammer blow to the knee, taking with it the sun, the blue sky, the little pink clouds and just about everything else. Now that these clear markers had been replaced by total darkness, with the exception of the stars, I could no longer get my direction from the sun as I'd done up to that point. It was most unfortunate that, despite the fact that during a brief period of my life I had nurtured some interest in the various Ptolemaic, Copernican and other systems and had seen the entire Star Wars saga several times, I had never learned to recognize the stars and constellations. They certainly did retain a poetic and romantic value for me, though this was not particularly useful at the moment.

I didn't let Boris in on any of this as I didn't want him to know about my momentary disorientation but, perhaps sensing that something was amiss, he suggested, "Why you not turn on satellite navigator?"

There are times when the greatest obstacles, upon closer examination, turn out to be as small and insignificant as a miserable little louse, and this was one of those times. Two hours later we were flying over Riversmill, where we could now land directly, seeing as Tatiana had abandoned us and we no longer had to accompany her to Mountainsmill. I asked myself just whom she might be entertaining at that very moment with her more or less witty humor. Aware of my limits as a pilot, I decided to land in a field just outside the city, far away from prying eyes. The problem, however, was that, while it was well out of the spotlight, it was also pot-holed, dark and damned short.

They say that fortune favors the brave, although the guy who launched himself off the peak of Everest on his bike and now rests in peace at the bottom of some gorge might disagree. The fact is that this time, the blindfolded goddess kept her concentration and did her duty right to the end. The wheels touched down in a huge pile of slimy manure which sent the plane skidding into an oak tree at the end of the field, but at least it was in one piece.

I was quite satisfied with myself, as we walked Indian file in the pale moonlight along the side of the road toward Riversmill. Boris, meanwhile, maintained his habitually indecipherable expression. The only one grumbling was the Siberian wolf.

I rang the doorbell at home at about three o'clock in the morning, but I knew Lorelai never went to bed before four. The only danger was that she might be listening to music with her headphones on and not hear the bell. Luckily this wasn't the case. She opened the door, wrapped up in her long, semi-transparent nightgown. As soon as she recognized me, she threw her arms around my neck, exclaiming, "Sweetie pie! Where have you been? I've been looking everywhere for you!"

"In Russia, doll-face. Later on I'll tell you all about it," I cut short. "I've brought a couple of friends with me."

Lorelai realized that I wasn't alone. Her mouth made that heart-shape it always does when she gets a surprise, and she exclaimed, "But that's Sergei Mussovrinski, and he's got a husky with him!"

"This no husky," Boris specified. "This Siberian wolf."

"How cute!" chirped Lorelai, a lover of all

animals. If you brought her a little squirrel, a walrus, or a crocodile, it wouldn't make the slightest difference to her. For her they were all "cute."

And wouldn't you know! This bad-tempered wolf that had done nothing but snarl and glare at me now changed his tune completely, going over to Lorelai and rubbing himself against her legs, asking to be petted like a kitten looking for affection.

Motivated perhaps by a touch of jealousy, I decided to interrupt this nascent idyll, saying gruffly, "Well Lorelai, are you going to let us in or do we have to stand out here all night?"

The wolf gave me one of his usual threatening stares, and we went inside.

CHAPTER 9

When we got to the living room, Lorelai and I sat down on the purple sofa, Boris curled up on a black and white checkered ottoman, and the wolf made himself right at home under the table, perhaps mistaking it for a cave in the Ural Mountains.

"So tell me just what happened to my wacky little sweetie pie," Lorelai said, smiling at Boris but referring to me. She simply couldn't get it into her head not to call me that, especially when we had company.

I didn't protest and proceeded to bring her up to speed on recent events. Although she was a bit of the emotional type, she only fainted three times, and when I'd finished, she got up and said, "I need something to help me recover. Do you two want something to drink? A cold lemonade, a hot lemonade, a green lemonade, a yellow lemonade, a lemonade up, a lemonade down, a lemonade here or a lemonade there?"

This was her way of being funny, but those who didn't know her were often taken aback.

Not the impassible Boris, though, who answered, "Me green lemonade, thank you." Caught off guard, Lorelai now had her work cut out for her concocting a glass of this mysterious beverage.

I waited for everyone to assume their positions, and then I began to explain my plan for catching the mad scientist Professor Von Strakken and his right-hand man, the treacherous postman Jonathan, guilty of having killed and frozen Sergei Mussovrinski. For it was to this end alone that I'd brought Boris and that delight of a Siberian wolf of his home from Russia. The plan hinged completely on the remarkable resemblance between Boris and Sergei Mussovrinski; I would have challenged their very mothers, if they'd ever had one, to distinguish between them.

My idea was to convince that nasty Von Strakken that Sergei Mussovrinski was still alive, and thus tempt him to try to kill him once more. The professor would thus be forced to reveal himself, just in time to fall into the trap which I would set for him and his deserving associate.

But in order for this to occur, it was necessary to spread the news of Sergei Mussovrinski's reappearance as widely as possible, so that it might reach the ears of the mad scientist.

I'd done some thinking about this during our plane trip and realized that the best thing would've been for Sergei Mussovrinski (a.k.a.

Boris) to get into the papers or, even better, on television. There were several ways to achieve this. Our hero perform some daring stunt, such as throwing himself from a skyscraper naked with his legs bound. He could save the prime minister who was about to be hit by a tram, or he himself could become prime minister. This last hypothesis, in my view, would guarantee the greatest visibility, the more so in that I knew some very influential people at the bocce club who assist us in this direction.

When I finished explaining my plan, there was a moment of silence interrupted almost immediately by Lorelai, who exclaimed with her usual uncontrollable enthusiasm, "What a diabolical plan! What an active imagination you have, my wonderful darling! That way we'll be able to hit two birds with one stone!"

"What stone?" asked Boris, who didn't seem to hold my plan in such high regard. "So we have two possibilities: either I be target for crazy killer, or I fall naked in front of tram. This plan not seem to me very good."

I would've liked to explain to him that he'd completely misunderstood the story about the tram, but he didn't give me the time. He stood up and said to the Siberian wolf, "Come Kazimir, we return to great Mother Russia."

Well, I finally learned the beast's name, but this was meagre consolation. Boris' sudden defection put the entire operation at risk.

I stood up as well and tried to convince him

to stay: "Boris, don't go! If it's a question of money, we'll find a solution. I'm willing to double my initial offer of twenty-five dollars. And you haven't even considered the third hypothesis - you could become prime minister!"

"Prime minister of dirty capitalist country! If mad scientist not kill me, someone else certainly kill me. Scientist not be crazy, you be crazy!"

The last person who 'd called me 'crazy', years ago, was still to this day wandering the streets in a daze after I got through slapping him around, but this time I tried to control myself, seeing as I was going to need that bearded Cossack. If, on the other hand, his wolf wanted to go back to Russia it was fine by me. I certainly wasn't going to stop him. But what I couldn't do was let someone call me crazy and pretend everything was hunky dory, so I shot back, "If I'm crazy, then you're a fool." It was a bit of an infantile reaction, I'll admit, but right there and then I was unable to come up with anything better. I must have touched a nerve, however, since Boris, abandoning his usual imperturbability, cried out: "Fool to me, nephew of Vladimir Stanislav Timuroff, grand chancellor at court of Tsar Nicholas II! If me fool, then you big shit!"

Nobody, and I mean nobody, had ever called me 'big shit,' and I felt the blood rush straight to my head. I was about to turn again into the hairy, sharp-toothed monster Grunz, when Lorelai intervened in the nick of time.

CHAPTER 10

It wasn't the first time that angel in girl's clothing was able to extinguish my blaze and make the best out of a bad situation. Though I was often so blind as to be unaware of it, the quality of my life had clearly improved since Lorelai had come into it.

"Be good, kids" she chirped. "And you, my furious little sweetie pie, put your claws away. You've just finished telling me so many wonderful things, but now brace yourself, because I've got some news to tell you as well."

My rage suddenly vanished and was replaced by the usual apprehension that gripped me every time Lorelai had any news to tell me. The last time I'd heard her say this, she'd gone on to reveal to me that she'd sold to a junk-collector that horrible little drawing hanging in the hallway that made her sick to her stomach every time she walked by it and, in her eyes, for a great price. Shame that what lay behind the frame was one of Picasso's first cubist sketches.

"Watch this," she said, opening the door to

the pool room, out of which leaped a crazed, possibly drunk monkey that began doing somersaults and generally running amok. In the course of his inopportune acrobatics, the pesky little quadrumane jumped on my back, on Lorelai's head (which amused her to no end), pulled Kazimir the wolf's tail (which inexplicably provoked no particular reaction), and finally gave Boris a nice pull on the beard, which unexpectedly fell away to reveal the clean-shaven face of Sergei Mussovrinski that I knew so well.

"Sergei!" I cried in amazement. "So it is you!"

"I not understand" he tried to say, but he could fool me no longer.

I grabbed him by the collar and began to shake him, just as I'd done the first time we met in that distant Russian port, and as I did then I yelled in his face, "Do you take me for a fool? Enough already! Out with it! What's the meaning of this charade!"

"Oh all right," said Sergei Mussovrinski, taking a seat on the ochre-colored couch with red stripes and lighting his pipe. "I'll tell you the whole story, from beginning to end." As a cloud of pestilential smoke enveloped him, hiding him almost completely from sight, he began his account: "You might have wondered what I was doing in that out-of-the way Russian port. Well, as soon as I found out Von Strakken's sentence was up in Cayenne, I knew right away he'd be out for revenge, so I made myself scarce. I hid out on an Indian reserve disguised as one of them, where thanks to my enthusiastic use of the peace pipe, I picked up this habit of smoking you may have noticed. But I still didn't feel completely safe, so I thought I'd get away even further, to the North Pole among the Eskimos, an extremely hospitable and cordial people, though a bit cold at first touch. I have to tell you that even the seals were not half-bad, but the ones I really couldn't stand were the walruses. You cannot imagine how unbearably irritating and boring they are! So I dressed up as a Cossack and went down to Russia. Imagine my surprise when I saw you appear in that far-off port. I decided that, in any event, it was better to not to reveal my true identity to you, if only for your own safety.

At this point Sergei Mussovrinski interrupted his account and took a few puffs of smoke from that sort of pipe-shaped incinerator, thanks to which the room was rapidly being covered by a mouse-gray patina, and then continued: "Before making my escape, I'd left a wax statue of myself in my apartment here in Riversmill in order to fool Von Strakken. If events have unfolded as I think they have, there won't be much left of that statue." I was amazed at the precision of this intuition of his, exclaiming, "And to think that I wanted to use *you* as the bait to catch Von Strakken!"

"If I'd known that was what you had in mind, I certainly wouldn't have come with you."

No one spoke for several minutes as I fell into a deep meditation. The situation was now radically different: Von Strakken, in spite of himself, hadn't killed anyone but a wax statue. Sergei Mussovrinski, though he was enveloped in a cloud of pestilential smoke, was alive and well. Lorelai was smiling at me, right here in front of me, as she stroked the bizarre head of that lice-ridden monkey. It thus seemed that, albeit in a slightly bizarre fashion, everything was getting back to normal.

When I came out of my trance, I asked Sergei, "By the way, where did you find the wolf? I assume you must have taken him for personal defense."

It was at this point that something incredible happened. Kazimir the wolf, who until now had remained aloof, came forward and rose up on his hind feet, saying: "Sergei, why don't you quit jerking your friend around and tell him the truth?"

He then opened the zipper running all the way down the front of his body and stripped off his fur coat. And who else emerged but him, just him, nobody else but him! What was the story here? What the devil was happening? I was struggling to believe my eyes and ears. And even if it seemed absurd, I wasn't hallucinating. I'll be damned if it wasn't him, just him, and nobody else. He laughed mockingly, just as he had when he'd sent me straight into the frigid waters of the river. It was Jonathan the postman!

CHAPTER 11

"Surprised, you turkey?" he said to me, and turning towards Sergei he added, "And you, what are you waiting for?"

So Sergei too opened the zipper that ran down his front, and I felt the blood freeze in my veins as I saw my friend turn into no less than his archenemy, Professor Von Strakken!

In just a few seconds everything had changed again, but this time for the worse, like when a large black cloud comes and suddenly obscures the most brilliant sunshine. Worse, in fact, since what was happening made absolutely no sense at all. I no longer knew what to do or what to think, because everything had happened too quickly and I was caught off guard. I looked at Lorelai, sitting there on the red and blue-striped couch with her mouth open and the monkey in her arms. She was still as a statue, but then suddenly her image fragmented, turning itself into a flock of white doves that began to fly in every direction. This was truly incredible - what else could possibly happen now? Then suddenly the furniture in the room, not wanting to be outdone, decided to join in the fun. The black and white, checkered otto-man got up on two legs, unzipped itself and out came a poodle. The couch did the same and out popped a camel. The table became a miniature of Chartres Cathedral and the mon-key Charlie Chaplin, with mustache, bowler and bamboo cane to boot. Then the whole room began to spin. I couldn't stay on my feet, eve-rything went dark, a blinding light flashed befo-re my eyes, or perhaps in my brain. For a mo-ment I saw my old wet nurse chasing me with a soup ladle, I felt something in my stomach, similar to being punched repeatedly, I received various revelations of the future of humanity, and finally I had the distinct sensation that all this had already happened, at which point I lost consciousness and felt lifeless to the floor.

When I awoke I had no idea how much time had passed, and it took me a while to realize where I was. The sun was blinding and the floor on which I was lying was unstable, as though atop the waves. I thought I might still be delirious, but little by little I came to realize I was in the middle of the ocean, lying once again on that worn-out wooden door on which I had already once awoken after having fallen into the river in my duel with that treacherous postman, Jonathan.

I sat down and looked around. There was nothing but water in every direction. I admit I was feeling rather confused, but these latest development would've disoriented even the most experienced sailor. In those moments, I was glad I'd taken that course in psycho-acrobatics with the yogi Tiburzio a few years back, which had so tempered my mind that it wasn't easily upset. I got to thinking and it didn't take me long to wrap my mind around what had happened. It was all the fault of that *karkàk*, the poison in which I'd dipped the two Malaysian daggers used in that stupid duel with Jonathan the postman. As I've already mentioned, *karkàk* is a hallucinogenic psycho-stimulator, and that was what had undoubtedly made me delirious , making me believe all these events had been real when they had only ever unfolded in my mind. Nothing had actually happened, and therefore, Sergei Mussovrinski's homicide was likewise still unsolved. Though, when it comes right down to it, who can really say where dreams end and so-called reality begins? Perhaps we'll wake up one day to discover that reality has been nothing but an extravagant dream.

These profound lucubrations succeeded in calming me down somewhat. Slowly but surely I relaxed, and began to appreciate the advantages of being lost at sea. I came to the conclusion that, all things considered, a week adrift can actually be quite pleasant, since it allows you to finally have a little time to yourself, enjoy some peace and quiet, and get your thoughts in order. The situation probably changes if that one week becomes two, three or more, particularly if the castaway in question has not taken the precaution of bringing along a good supply of victuals and a decent sun cream.

And thus my days initially passed, placid and serene, until I had a sort of *déjà-vu*, and that is, that something happened to me that I sensed I had already experienced. I saw a dot on the horizon that did not appear to be, as it seems to me I've already said on another occasion, one of the usual whales in the habit of scurrying back and forth across the ocean. This was definitely something different. And the closer it came, the less it resembled a whale and the more it resembled that thing that every respectable castaway hopes to see appear on the horizon (I believe I may have already said this as well).

Now I'm not someone who is easily amazed; but when that 'thing' was close enough for me to recognize it, I must confess it succeeded in raising my eyebrows.

It was a battle ship, and from the stern Lorelai, her face illuminated by a smile that stretched from ear to ear, was waving her arms to greet me.

As soon as I came on board, I took her in my arms and asked her, "My little desert fox, would you mind explaining to me …" but she cut me off, put her tapered finger over my mouth and told me with a chirp, "Seeing as you bought it, I thought I might as well use it. And that's not all, my crazy little sweetie pie, because you ought to know I've been able to sell it back to that junk dealer at the end of the road, and I even made a little profit." It came to mind that, all things considered, there was a little brain under that cloud of blond hair that wasn't half-bad, and I told her so. She began to dance and it seemed as though she were dancing on a cloud.

And thus, while the battle ship slid lazily across the water towards a sunset that seemed to want to set the sky on fire, I snatched that dancing fairy queen out of the sky, pulled her towards me, and kissed her on those strawberry-colored lips.

EPISODE 2

AN INTRIGUING GUEST

CHAPTER 1

For three days that car had been parked in front of my house, and I didn't like it one bit. I wasn't even able to make out who was sitting at the wheel since the windows were closed and the inside was full of smoke. Most likely it was a Turk, or at least someone who smoked like a Turk; or possibly a Londoner, who had decided to bring some of his city's fog along with him. In any case, a cop it surely was not. I'd called Lieutenant Bolfon, a friend of mine down at Homicide, and he'd assured me no policeman would have any interest in hanging around this neighborhood, the western side of the hill to the east of the central park of Riversmill, a generally quiet area apart from the werewolf who, from time to time, appeared in the park on nights of a full moon.

Thus, from behind the curtains I was watching the man who had come to watch me, when Lorelai called to tell me that our dinner had once again gone up in smoke, and that therefore it would be necessary to eat out yet again. I was beginning to suspect she was doing it on purpose. It was simply not possible that that girl could burn our dinner practically every evening. There were only two possibilities: either she was damned stupid or damned smart, and I knew that little blond was far from stupid, even if she liked to make people think otherwise. But I had no desire to play the fool either, so I whipped up a little spread of canned sardines, salad, and hardboiled eggs. On the third consecutive evening that I presented her with this same meagre offering, Lorelai gave up and moaned, embracing me and rearranging my hair, "My crazy little sweetie pie, do we have to eat this horrible stuff every night?"

We thus came to an agreement and the armistice was signed. We would go out to eat every other day; the evenings we stayed in, we would trade off in the kitchen. She certainly got the better of the deal, since in a previous life I had been head chef in the kitchens of Charlemagne, a.k.a. the Great Gobbler.

Anyhow, the problem was resolved and domestic harmony returned.

One evening I was in the green parlor, ensconced in the velvet armchair with the Hohenzollern arms on it. For some hours I had been taking great pleasure in reading the conclusive documents from the 1815 Congress of Vienna, when Lorelai brought me back to reality, saying with her chirpy voice, "My erudite little sweetie pie, it's your turn to cook tonight and we're all out of unripe cucumber juice."

This was terrible news. For it could only mean one thing, and that was that someone had to go out and get some more at Gunnar the Swede's corner shop. I had no desire at all to leave the house, given that the rain was coming down in such a way that Noah with his Ark would have felt perfectly at home, so I replied, almost without looking up from the old volume of yellowed pages I was reading, "There might be a couple of bottles in the trunk at the end of the hallway of arms." Lorelai, however, was quick to dash my hopes: "Don't be silly, lemon pie. You know very well it was you who gulped down the very last one this morning."

At this point my hopes were definitely scattered, like a swarm of mosquitos approaching a fumigator.

First sweetie pie and now lemon pie: Lorelai simply refused to stop calling me these ridiculous names, and the worst part about it was that, slowly but surely, I was getting used to it. In any case, a dinner without unripe cucumber juice was no dinner at all, and seeing as my innate sense of chivalry prevented me from sending Lorelai out to brave the storm, I put down the book, got up, put on my extra-large yellow raincoat, grabbed the big umbrella, and fearlessly ventured out into the tempest.

Gunnar the Swede's shop wasn't far away, on the corner at the end of street, in front of the Egyptian stele. In normal weather conditions it would've taken me no more than five minutes to get there, but on this evening I had to grapple with an honest-to-goodness downpour. So much water was coming down that I was amazed I didn't bump into anyone in a diving suit or, at the very least, with a mask and flippers. The wind made me skid and I staggered forward like a drunkard. Between the darkness and the water, I could barely see anything and so failed to realize that I was unintentionally approaching the car that had been parked in front of my house for three days. Suddenly, a bolt of lightning tore through the dark and lit up for a moment the face of the man sitting at the wheel. The wind then blew me away again, this time in the right direction towards Gunnar's shop. I purchased a couple of bottles of unripe cucumber juice and then proceeded to throw myself back out into the storm, succeeding I don't know exactly how in making my way back to our door. Yet, when I was buying the bottles of juice, during my return home, and as I was coming into the vast, torch-lit entry way and going back up the long, stone staircase, leaving a trail of water in my wake, I couldn't get out of my mind the image of that face the lightning bolt had so briefly revealed to me. Though I tried everything to convince myself I was mistaken and hadn't seen clearly, inside of me there was no doubt, for the image had planted itself crystal clear in my mind. At the same time, however, it wasn't something I could easily accept. No, it was not at all easy to accept something this absurd, and that is, that the man behind the wheel in that car was … me!

CHAPTER 2

Though I had witnessed many - too many - strange things in my life, this crazy world never ceased pulling something totally new out of its hat to amaze me. When I got back home Lorelai jumped down from the large, multicolored wooden rocking horse we kept in the entry way and came towards me. Thanks to her sixth or perhaps even seventh sense, she immediately realized there was something strange about me, not least because I had put my raincoat in the refrigerator and the juice bottles in the dresser.

She stood in front of me, hands on her hips, her foot rhythmically tapping the ground, and as she looked me up and down with that little teasing smile of hers, she asked, "So let's hear it, what is it this time?"

One of the things that made living with Lorelai possible and which had convinced me to repudiate my lone-wolf nature was the fact that, with her, I could talk about anything. It simply would never occur that she not believe something I said, or consider it too bizarre. In short, we were in sync. So I told her what I'd seen. Right then and there, she rubbed her eyes to the point that she resembled a young owl taking his first look at the world around him, then she exclaimed: "Oh, come on! How can you be at the wheel of that car, if you're right here?"

This reaction of hers might seem to contradict what I've just said about our being in sync, but in reality, far from doubting my story, she was merely pointing to the fact that it was illogical. On the other hand, how could you blame her? I fell onto the Empire-style couch, saying, "I need to think for a moment."

"Why don't you think while we eat?" she proposed, taking me by the hand and helping me back to my feet. "While you were out there braving the storm, I prepared dinner."

What an angel! It wasn't even her turn. I followed her towards the sumptuously laid table, my heart full of gratitude and willing to turn a blind eye to the imperfect manner in which she had hurriedly gone about setting it. If I had dared set Charlemagne's table in such a way, "the Great Gobbler" would surely have had me hung in a cage from the walls of Aachen to rot. But of course, those were different times.

Despite the fact that the eggs-on-a-stick and banana soufflé were truly superb, I had no appetite and was content to pick at things here and there, such that, as we were finishing up,

Lorelai took the soufflé and poured it over my head. As I was cleaning myself up in the bathroom, she asked me, candidly leaning against the door frame, "So, my greasy little sweetie pie, now that you've given it a good thinking, what have you concluded?"

"It's obvious," I replied. "I'm going back down to have another look."

"Good, I think you'll see you were mistaken."

Though the rain had now stopped, I once again put on my extra-large yellow raincoat, in whose inside pocket, just to avoid any misunderstandings, I placed my trusty oblong, double-barreled, carbon-reinforced Fergusson K16 pistol, and set off toward the door.

"Are you coming with me?" I asked Lorelai before going out.

"No no, you go. You'll tell me all about it. After all, someone has to clear the table."

When I got down to the street there was a totally different atmosphere compared to the first time. There were still some raindrops coming down, but these were dripping off the leaves and the edges of the roofs. The famous "calm after the storm" was now everywhere, not to be confused with the one before. There wasn't a soul in sight. I approached the car, parked under a street lamp, from the rear. My intention was to knock on the driver's window and clear up matters once and for all, and I did just that. When, shortly thereafter, Lorelai saw me come back inside, she was even more surprised at my appearance than the first time. I must have looked really strange, since she asked me, "Did you go to the hairdresser, or did your hair stand up on end all but itself? Who was in the car this time, Count Dracula?"

Poor dear, she had no way of knowing that if that kooky old Count Dracula I had met years ago in Transylvania had been there, there wouldn't have been any problem - but the truth was otherwise.

"This is big, this is really big!" I repeated, walking back and forth across the parlor. Thinking I was talking about her mouth (she had this complex about her lips being too big, which was absolutely not true), Lorelai frowned and even shed a tear, but fortunately this misunderstanding was immediately cleared up.

I was quite nervous, however, and as I often did when my nerves got the better of me, I took my red bicycle out of the closet and started pedaling around like a madman on my own personal obstacle course in and around the furniture. Lorelai found this habit unbearable. For, as almost always happened, I ended up breaking something and this time, it was the 9th century Ming-Ting-Tong vase I'd acquired in the far-off kingdom of the flying foxes of Chin-Chun, from which I'd transported it by sled to the Li-Pa-Tan border.

While Lorelai helped me pick up the pieces and raved about improbable repairs with the help of the fantastic ceramic glues available at Gunnar's store, I grabbed her suddenly by the wrist. She immediately froze, and as she looked at me with surprise, her big blue eyes wide open, I asked her, "Do you want to know who was at the wheel of the car?"

"Wait a moment," she answered. "Let me guess. I like guessing games ...," and after a moment she threw out a few names: "Gunnar? Your Aunt Domitilla? Igor Stravinsky? Mickey Mouse? Santa Clause? David Bowie?"

"No," I told her. "It was you."

CHAPTER 3

Lorelai began to laugh. For a while she was unable to stop, but then, drying her tears, she said to me, "I'm sorry, my delusional little sweetie pie, but how can I be down in that car when I'm up here instead? Or do you mean that I'm not here, but I only think I am while I'm really down in that car?"

It was a fascinating theory, but now wasn't the time to mull it over. I put on my extra-large raincoat for the third time and set off once again toward the door, exclaiming, "Enough is enough! We've already put it off for too long!"

A moment later I was in the street, and the next I had thrown the car door wide open, shouting, "Out of the car immediately! The game is up!"

I didn't know who I was about to confront, but I was ready for anything. There emerged a wrinkled, hunched-over old woman, dressed in black with a black shawl, and a little black cap complete with veil. She reach out to me with the hand she wasn't using to hold her cane and asked me with a shrill voice, "Young man, are you going to help me cross the street or not?"

My sense of chivalry demanded I immediately grant her request, leaving momentarily to the side all doubts and questions which that unexpected apparition had aroused. Once we reached the opposite sidewalk, she raised the point of her cane and, pointing at my door, told me imperiously, "Let's go to your house!"

Normally, I do not blindly obey the first command given to me by a total stranger, even if they are elderly and wobbly on their feet, and thus I had a moment of hesitation, but she resolutely pushed me in the direction she'd indicated. I decided to play along since it seemed that would be the only way to get some answers. As we climbed the long, stone staircase, I was quite amazed by the extraordinary agility of that old woman, so fragile and unsteady at first glance.

When we came inside, though she treated the woman with the utmost regard and politeness, Lorelai never took her eyes off of her; from her expression, it was as if I had brought home a skunk or something similar. More than once she secretly gave me quizzical looks in the hopes of an explanation I couldn't give her.

But the explanation was not long in coming. As we sipped the tea Lorelai had most opportunely served in the blue parlor, silence reigned supreme. A cordially embarrassed atmosphere had been created in which no one dared to speak. Every now and then our eyes crossed, but this generated only timid smiles of circumstance. But then, all of a sudden, the little old woman rose to her feet, her eyes lit up, her hair changed from white to red, and she picked up her cane and devoured it completely. "If you wanted some cookies, all you had to do was as...," Lorelai tried to say, but I motioned her to be silent. The old witch then completed a series of movements similar to a Maori dance and, finally, went as stiff as a frozen cod, a state in which she remained for several seconds. In that very moment the doorbell rang, and I had to go see who was there. It was the postman, come to deliver the prize we had won with our collection of milk-points - a ridiculous plush ear-warmer! His timing really could not have been any better! Luckily, when I returned the frozen cod - *alias* the old woman - was still there. Little by little, her image began to dissolve and in its place there appeared a beautiful young woman with red hair, green skin, and eyes of gold. She wore a skin-tight silver uniform. Lorelai put her hands on her hips and said, frowning at me, "And who might this be? An old friend of yours? Why did you bring her here?"

This didn't seem to me the best moment for a jealous tirade and I told her to calm down. The green young woman sat down and began to speak with a melodious voice, a far cry from old woman's shrill cackle: "I apologize for the trouble I am causing you. My name is Petulla."

"The word is 'petulant'," Lorelai shot back dryly, but I covered her mouth with my hand, getting lipstick all over it in the process.

"I come from the planet Flipflap, and I am a mutant."

"The word is 'mutilation'," Lorelai interrupted again, once I'd removed my hand from her mouth. Her hostility toward the new arrival was as clear as day.

"I can take on any shape you desire."

"Even that of a teeny, weeny mouse?" Lorelai asked her, with a ferocious expression that was not very reassuring. I reminded her she was no Puss 'n Boots.

"My spaceship has broken down and I am looking for someone to help me repair it."

"We can look in the Yellow Pages," said Lorelai, making as if to get up and look for it. "There must be a spaceship mechanic nearby."

I stopped her and immediately offered that beautiful extraterrestrial my unconditional assistance. My abovementioned sense of chivalry wouldn't allow me to neglect a damsel with a broken-down spaceship in the middle of the vast universe. This completely disinterested gesture of mine, however, cost me a kick in the shins from Lorelai. My first instinct, probably deriving from having spent a long period of my youth in a harsh academy in Siberia where you had to fight to the death for every crust of bread, was to pay her back in kind, and with interest, but I was able to restrain myself thanks to an equally long period subsequently spent in the monastery of Pi-Po, where I'd learned to control my reactions within reasonable limits.

So I pretended nothing had happened and asked Petulla, "Where's your spaceship now?" and she replied, "It is not far. It is the car parked down there, under the streetlamp."

CHAPTER 4

I could not believe my ears.

"But that's not possible. That's a perfectly normal car!" I exclaimed.

"Just like me, the spaceship too" she explained, "had mutant powers, and before it broke down I had transformed it to fit in with your primitive vehicles."

I wasn't fond of the term 'primitive,' and neither was Lorelai, who got up and left us, saying, "Please excuse me while I go get my bear club. I'll be right back."

Fearing she might be serious and return to give us both a good bashing in the head, I decided to speed things up.

"Come on, Petulla" I said, "let's go take a look at your car."

"You pronounce my name so well," replied the gorgeous alien, getting up and approaching me with her cat-walk, "You humans certainly are intriguing, and you more than anyone."

Fortunately, Lorelai had gone. In any case I decided to ignore this, put on my extra-large raincoat, and asked her to follow me. But as soon as I opened the door, I heard Lorelai exclaim: "Where are you going? I'm coming too," and immediately after I saw her come running up, having already put on her fuchsia-colored jacket.

She was very nervous. Her purse fell three times in quick succession, then her lipstick, her coin purse, her sunglasses, her phone, a glass, a fork, a spoon, a hair dryer, a mixer, a grass trimmer, and a bowling ball.

I took her aside and asked, "Would you mind telling me what's wrong with you? I've never seen you so nervous."

"Nervous? What are you talking about? You're the one who's nervous, my treacherous little sweetie pie. I couldn't be more normal."

She had clearly taken things the wrong way and was getting all bent out of shape. I should also add that her jealousy was totally unjustified, since although the green alien was undoubtedly quite beautiful, in my eyes Lorelai was much more so, and in every sense of the word. But things had already gotten off on the wrong foot. I thought about how to resolve the situation, and it seemed like a good idea that while I went down to the street to take a look at the car, the girls stay inside and get to know each other better and become friends. This plan did not please either of them, but I wasn't about to put it to a vote, so whether they liked it or not, they had to do as I said. As soon as I was alone I knew the plan, at least from my point of view, had been the right one. Oh blessed solitude! I generally don't turn down the company of females, but too much is too much.

I'd brought along the keys to the car and my toolbox, but now that I was alone, I could also be honest with myself and admit there wasn't much hope of my being able to repair the spaceship. Even though the vehicle seemed like a normal car from top to bottom, it really wasn't at all. Petulla had explained to me that by turning the key to the left, the entire spaceship would assume its true shape and the internal-combustion engine would turn back into an ion-photonic, tetra-dimensional one, that is, the type of engine whose name I couldn't even pronounce. I sat down in the driver's seat and inserted the key, but before turning it, I stopped for a moment to gaze up at the sky. The air was clear, the clouds had disappeared, and the stars were vying to see which of them could shine the brightest. I took a deep breath and was pervaded by a profound sense of peace. This was the famous "calm before the storm," not to be confused the one after it. The storm was indeed not long in coming, and it was sparked by something of no particular importance, a trifle, mere forgetfulness. Petulla had simply neglected to inform me that, before turning the key, it was necessary to de-activate the alarm which, wouldn't you know, was one of the few things still functioning on the spaceship. And moreover, if there was one thing that on her planet was as well-regarded as a kick in the teeth and, therefore, severely punished, more or less like horse theft in the time of the cowboys, it just happened to be the theft of a spaceship. I thus naively turned the key to the left as I'd been told and, a moment later, I found myself decomposed into molecules, launched onto a far-off prison planet in the Orion galaxy, and there recomposed and ready to serve my sentence.

The place was a nightmare. What little of the landscape you could see in that semi-darkness was arid and bleak as can be, and a sad, depressing music, a sort of melancholy howl perhaps created by the wind, pervaded the heavy, suffocating air.

Right there and then I didn't understand what had happened, but of one thing I was sure: *something* had certainly happened. Suddenly finding myself in such a horrible place made me initially think that I'd died and gone to hell; in which case I was determined to file a complaint. Now I've certainly been no saint, but those seven hundred or more political prisoners I'd broken out of Strotzenplok Prison some ten years before ought to have earned some points in my favor.

So I wandered around those dark, desolate lands in search of an explanation, until I saw a tiny light far off in the distance, and remembering what Hansel and Gretel had done in similar circumstances, I set off hopeful in that direction.

CHAPTER 5

Unlike in the fable, however, I didn't find a house made of marzipan and candied fruit. First of all, that tiny light was really very far away and it was no brief stroll to get there. I had to cross vast, moonlike expanses, barriers of dense thorns and sharp canes of bamboo, foul-smelling swamps, and all this while enveloped in a semi-darkness that would have disoriented even a carrier pigeon with a compass. Despite these difficulties, I was finally able to reach my destination, only to discover that that light was the miserable little fire of a man who, at first sight, seemed to be an old vagrant. He wore tattered clothes and had a long white beard that hung down to his feet. Seated in front of that little fire, he was warming up some beans in a battered little pot.

"Do you want some?" he asked me.

I accepted, and while we ate he got up and began to walk back and forth, rapt, tripping from time to time on his beard which was continually getting tangled up between his legs. Then he sat down again and began to speak …

about me. He told me who I was and how I'd arrived there; he explained to me the story of the anti-theft alarm and my transfer onto that planet, he unveiled our present location, and he also told me what numbers to play in the lottery. My mouth was agape, but he suggested I close it. Just who was this miserable-looking man who seemed to know everything about everything? When I asked him, he replied, "I am Kaspar, and I have been here for 742 years. I was imprisoned for stealing my classmate's snack in second grade, and ever since, I have lived in complete solitude."

Despite the injustice of his case, he had a serene and tranquil expression with no sign of resentment. I found this man fascinating.

"I understand" I said. "But how've you managed to go on alone for all this time?"

"First I despaired, then I went insane, later I wisened up, and finally I began to meditate, given that I certainly had the time. When my mind reached the confines of the universe, which by the way do not exist, I no longer desired to leave, so I stayed put. Would you like to become my disciple?"

What a bizarre proposal! I thought about it for a moment, and then replied, "Why not?"

I stayed with him for five years and learned many things, such as how to balance on your pinkies for six hours, see with your ears, listen with your nose and other such things, though I was never able to learn to use telepathy which he, on the other hand, knew quite well. Kaspar often told me I was a dunce and I returned the favor, calling him a dope for always tripping over his beard. One day, that wise guy took a scissors to his beard and solved the problem at the root. But now I had nothing with which to parry his thrusts when he called me a dunce, so I decided to leave. I asked him if there was a way to do so, and he revealed that my sentence had already ended two years before and thus I could leave whenever I chose. All I needed to do was to visit the Release Office. Release Office? What the heck was that? And so I discovered that beyond the mountain which took great joy in darkening our skies with its threatening shadow was an entire city called Pandemonium populated by other 'prisoners.' I couldn't believe my ears. So this harsh hermitical life we'd been living with its continual struggles and deprivation wasn't the only option on this damned planet! Within only a few hours' walk, there existed a city complete with electricity, running water and all the rest. Out of respect, I decided not to choke Kaspar to death, given that at this point he was practically my guru. I said goodbye and set off toward civilization.

I don't understand why certain hermits are so frugal with words - or better, perhaps I do, since after seven hundred or more years in which you don't see a single living soul, your conversational skills are no longer what they once were. But for Pete's sake, Kaspar might have alerted me to the fact that the city wasn't named Pandemonium by accident! Chaos reigned supreme in that God-forsaken metropolis. People were running pell-mell like frightened horses, or beating each other to the point that every two or three-hundred meters, vicious fights were breaking out. From the roofs these carefree delinquents got their kicks by throwing tiles down on the heads of helpless passersby. The only positive note was that no one seemed to possess firearms. Now I better understood Kaspar's choice to live away from all this, and I was grateful to him for having kept me far from this looney bin. Zigzagging my way through scraps, brawls and roof tiles falling from on high, I succeeded in finding the Release Office rather quickly, and it was lucky I did, for upon my arrival some lunatic was in the process of tearing off the sign.

Inside the building the atmosphere was completely different. Everything was clean and orderly, and a smiling young woman invited me to approach the desk where she was sitting. I started to speak but she cut me off. "You do not need to say anything; you were scanned upon entering the door. If your sentence were not up and if, most importantly, you were not completely reformed, having now become good and honest, you would not have been able to come in."

She proceeded to look at her computer

screen. "Here is your file: spaceship theft."

I told her there had been a judicial error.

"An error?" she said amazed, "Then why did you not appeal to the Grand Jury?"

"What Grand Jury?"

"The wise hermit, who knows all and has the power to free the innocent immediately. But it is of no importance now – you are free."

She pushed the red button on the desk in front of her and a green ray shone down on me from above. Before I was decomposed into molecules, however, I was quick enough to ask her, "Which wise hermit?" and hear her response, "Kaspar."

CHAPTER 6

A moment later, I rematerialized in front of my house with my extra-large yellow raincoat on and the toolbox in my hand, no different from when I'd left. It was early morning and the sun was blinding, as my eyes were no longer accustomed to so much light. So I used one of the tricks good old Kaspar had taught me -I looked around with my ears, and listened with my nose to the little birds that were chirping happily on the tree branches. There is no one more poetic, no one more inclined to appreciate the simple beauties of nature than the man just freed from prison. I felt the same intense sensations I'd already experienced in Scotland at the end of thirteen long years of imprisonment in the dark, dank dungeons of Norkham Castle after the failed MacLoren revolt. After a while, my eyes became re-accustomed to the light and I could transfer my senses back to their correct places of residence.

It was not without a feeling of relief that I noted that the spaceship-car was no longer

there, a sign that Petulla had been able to repair it and return home. My thoughts ran to
Lorelai. Poor thing, to think how she must have
suffered for me during these five years! To
think what her restless little brain must have
dreamed up! Who knows, perhaps she thought
I'd run away, enrolled in the Foreign Legion, or,
in the grip of a mystical crisis, taken refuge in
some Shinto monastery; or perhaps that I'd
been kidnapped or even killed by a fanatical
sect. Who knows what might have popped into
that silly little head of hers! I couldn't wait to
reassure her, but seeing as it was still very early and she was surely still asleep, I decided first to go to the newsstand and take a peek at
the papers to find out what day it was. When I
reached the Art Nouveau-style kiosk at the
head of the boulevard, I was distracted by the
headlines which, as usual, announced the most
absurd and catastrophic news in big block let-
ters. Poor journalists, they had to eat too! I
thus discovered that scientists believed the col-
lapse of Mount Everest and the consequent
overflowing of all the world's oceans to be imminent, a crocodile at the zoo was suffering
from a small case of indigestion after having
devoured a man weighing one hundred and
forty kilos, the prime minister had been caught
stealing money out of a sleeping beggar's hat,
and the first-place soccer team was planning to
buy a new player for three-hundred thousand
million billion. Hell! At least during my long im-

prisonment I hadn't had to choke down this nonsense! Finally I decided to look at the date of a newspaper, and if I hadn't previously become impervious to surprises, I would've been startled to see printed the date of the day following the one in which I had gone down to repair the spaceship. I looked at the other papers as well for confirmation, and they were all in agreement. Incredible! While for me five years had gone by, here only a few hours had passed. I knew all about space-time relativity, but it's one thing to know it in theory; banging your nose against it is a different matter altogether.

A question immediately struck me. How had Petulla managed to repair the spaceship and clear out in a single night? Something didn't add up, so I ran home, climbed the stairs three at a time, opened the door, and ran to the bedroom to see if by chance Lorelai had also been launched onto some far-off planet in a distant galaxy. Fortunately, my fears were unfounded. Lorelai was sleeping peacefully on our canopied bed, resting sweetly on the sheets like a forest nymph transferred only momentarily into the city. I went into the parlor and collapsed on the purple couch. All of a sudden, five years of exhaustion hit me at once and I fell into a deep sleep. I dreamed I was at a masquerade ball in Venice. At a certain point the guests removed their costumes and I discovered they were all aliens, all except for one, Kaspar, who said to me, "Watch out, there's a fly in the soup!"

I asked him, "What soup?" and he answered, "You dunce!"

When Lorelai woke me with a cry of surprise, it seemed that ten minutes had gone by, but in truth, it had been only five.

"Where have you been?" she asked me. "You never came back last night. Petulla went down to look for you, and she disappeared as well."

"And you didn't come looking for me?" I asked, sitting up and rubbing my eyes.

"I certainly did, but she went out to the street a moment before me. When I stuck my head out, there was no sign of her, you, or the car."

I told her what had happened to me and she exclaimed, "Five years? That moron! How can you forget something as important as the alarm? She deserves to have her head cut off and her body fed to the jackals!"

Such invective seemed to me frankly excessive. Never had I heard such harsh words come out of Lorelai's mouth, but I assumed it must have been due to a lethal mix of resentment and jealousy.

For the first time since Lorelai and I had been together, the mood in the house grew sullen. I tried to lighten things up by showing her a couple of the exercises I had learned from Kaspar, like balancing on your pinkies and the moving your ears without touching them, but to no avail.

"How stupid!" she declared, and she turned away from me and went back into the bedroom. I took it badly at first, but then I lay back down on the couch thinking that at least I was back home, the question was resolved, and the entire matter could easily be laid to rest.

CHAPTER 7

But that wasn't the case at all; something wasn't right. Lorelai had changed. She'd begun to cook better than usual, but that was no compensation for the fact that she'd become cold and distant, and more unpleasant as well. The cracks in our partnership seemed to be growing by the day, but this didn't seem to displease or disturb her any more than if a little wandering fly had taken a walk on her knee.

I was doing my best to ignore it, but I couldn't help but note the difference. I realized I even missed those ridiculous names she used to call me, like 'sweetie pie,' 'pumpkin,' and so forth. No more smiles, passing kisses, or sudden, unexpected embraces. And if I tried to make the first move, her expression would freeze me in my tracks as she pulled away. But what struck me most was that I never saw her dance anymore, whereas before she was always twirling around, even while she brushed her teeth or fried a couple of eggs. My thoughts returned nostalgically to the nights we used to go up into the tower and she danced in the moonlight while I played the balalai-ka; those long winter evenings when, curled up on the Chippendale couch near the fireplace, we read the poetry of Albrecht of Magdeburg, or went down to the projection room to watch the old films of Pappo and Manolito, laughing ourselves to tears. I also recalled that time I brought her a necklace from Africa which turned out to have been cursed by a witchdoctor; as soon as she put it on, she shrunk by 20 centimeters, and for the next month she slept inside a drawer of the night table.

So many wonderful memories! But it was all so different now; Lorelai spent hours and hours locked in the red room doing who knows what, and when she came out she was covered in dirt and spattered with paint, having locked the door behind her. If I asked her what she was up to, she'd respond, "Mind your own business!"

Even though I hated to admit it, I was feeling a bit down in the dumps. In order to forget my sadness, I immersed myself in the study of subatomic nanoparticles, their relationship with the cosmic winds, and the influence that these may have had on the ethereal bodies of penguins during the *aurora borealis*. But despite finding this topic exceedingly interesting, something inside was telling me that this wasn't the time to abandon reality, but rather to keep my eyes wide open, because there was something very important I had yet to grasp. Every now and then, I remembered Kaspar telling me, "Careful! There's a fly in your soup" and when I asked him "What soup?" he replied, "You dunce!"

One night, I went for stroll in the park to clear my head. It was late and I hadn't realized there was a full moon. If I hadn't been so depressed, I would've never forgotten that it was better not to loiter in the park on nights of a full moon, since it was then that the werewolf loved to run amok in those parts. And wouldn't you know it - soon after I saw him pop out in front of me from behind a bench, with his evil smile and his less than cordial manners. Not that this was an excessively serious problem for me. Every time someone attacked me or made me angry, sending the blood rushing to my head, for three minutes I would turn into the hairy, sharp-toothed monster Grunz, and when this occurred the situation tended to resolve itself quickly. That night, however, I paid the price for feeling so down in the dumps, because the transformation which had always been so instantaneous took place only after our dear friend had sunk his bothersome fangs into my thigh. Moreover, if I had transformed immediately I wouldn't have even needed to fight because when that mangy wolf saw the superiority of his opponent, he would surely have fled with his tail between his legs. But the die had now been cast and conflict was inevitable. While neither of us had anything to gain by attracting attention to ourselves, we nevertheless made such a racket that someone threw a shoe from the window of one of the houses overlooking the park. They must have taken us for a couple of quarrelsome alley cats.

Despite the fact that from the beginning the outcome of our struggle was never in any doubt, that pest of a wolf fought courageously and gave his best effort before finally raising the white flag and retreating. I knew his true identity quite well. His name was Robert, and when we were our normal selves we were great friends. He was the last descendent of an old family of painters, sculptors and musicians in which an undeniable artistic talent, in addition to the hereditary defect of lycanthropy, had been passed down from father to son. Just as mine had, his family had lived for generations in one of those venerable abodes near the park, and our respective fathers, grandfathers, and great-grandfathers had, in their time, also been involved in more or less ferocious battles with each other.

In any case, the fight was good for me and helped me to release some of the nervous tension I'd accumulated, clouding my mind and preventing me from seeing things clearly. Once I regained my normal appearance, I was once again afflicted, however, by that terrible headache which was an inevitable consequence of my transformation into the monster Grunz. The only way to get some relief was to bash my head against a wall; but with no walls to be found in the vicinity, I had to settle for a tree, after which I sat down on a bench to reflect.

"Poor Robert," I thought, "it can't be pleasant to have to turn into a louse-ridden, snap-happy wolf with every full moon. Who would ever think that, behind the wild and violent appearance of that wolf-man, there lies in reality the noble soul of a sensitive artist! It just goes to show that appearances can be deceiving, and what we see on the outside may not correspond with what lies within."

It was this thought that removed the veil from my eyes, the good fortune which emerged from an only apparently regrettable encounter and Robert's great merit! Making it clear to me now that a person could seem to be someone while, in reality, they were someone else. Finally, the mystery unravelled! How could I have been so blind! If Lorelai seemed to have suddenly become a different person, it wasn't because her tastes or behavior had changed, but rather because she was truly someone else. And what she was, to be precise, was a damned mutant that for some unknown purpose had had the bright idea of taking her place.

CHAPTER 8

The blood once again rushed to my head and a moment later I was already running home on four legs, having turned into the hairy, sharp-toothed monster Grunz. Fortunately, as I climbed the stone staircase five steps at a time, I had a chance to mull things over, such that when I got to the top I had already reassumed my normal appearance. In the nick of time, too, for there I ran into Lorelai, or, better, Petulla, who was just going out.

Bored and looking meaner than ever, she said to me, "Oh, it's you."

Only ten minutes earlier this attitude of hers would've had the same effect on me as having to swallow an ostrich egg whole, but now that I knew the truth it only made the blood rush to my head once more. I was able to control myself, however, and went inside, closing the door behind me as she went out. I had decided to be diplomatic so as not to put Lorelai's life at risk. Come to think of it, where was Lorelai? Had she too been sent to some far-off planet? Was she perhaps languishing down in the cel-

92

lar, having been locked up in the family crypt? Had she been sent to Turkey to look after sheep? I locked myself in the hexagonal room, the one with the white and turquoise marble floor, and began to pace back and forth on the large carpet given to me as a gift by the Maharajah Abu Babu Bebo. First, I had to discover what Petulla was up to in the red room. On second thought, no, first, I had to try to calm down, so I drank a few liters of chamomile tea from the samovar I'd been given by the Maharajah Abu Babu Bebo's cousin, the Caliph Babebo Babù Bebò.

I had to get into the red room without the wicked mutant noticing, and the only way to do so was to come in through the window. We were on the second floor, however, and so to reach it I had to make my way out on the ledge. Now that Petulla was gone there wasn't a moment to lose. I went out through one of the big, arc-shaped windows in the hexagonal room, but as soon as I was outside, a gust of wind slammed it closed. Now there could be no turning back. As I made my way forward along the 20 centimeter-wide ledge, I remembered that it was just down below there that I kept the tank full of the piranhas my cousin Frederick sent me every now and then from Colombia. What's more, I'd never quite understood why he did so, given that I'd never asked him for any. I got to the window of the red room but found it impossible to open. I peered through the glass and glimpsed a sort of enormous robot in the shape of a crab. I was just starting to look in my jacket pocket for my mini-binoculars when Petulla entered the room and closed the curtains, thus obliging me to retreat. The game was up. Unable to ask her to let me in or re-enter the way I'd come out, I had no choice but to stay out there, standing erect with my back against the wall like a tin soldier. As if that weren't enough, several pigeons came to press certain right of theirs for the exclusive use of the ledge, and an ant delegation came to protest because I was impeding their customary processions. At this point it began to pour. The rain lasted all night until at dawn the sky finally cleared, and I could thus spend a quite pleasant day standing up there on the ledge. I'd reached a compromise with the pigeons - I moved over a little to the right and they accepted me, almost unanimously, into their flock. The ants, on the other hand, were less open to strangers and continued their muttering.

Even though, ultimately, standing out there on the ledge was an experience like many others, I had no interest at all in getting into the Guinness' Book of Records. It was thus clear the experience couldn't go on for much longer. The priority was saving Lorelai and there was no time to lose. If only the hexagonal room's large windows hadn't been of such magnificent, Art-Nouveau stained-glass! Having to break one of them to get back inside was too painful to think about. I nevertheless approached the first of them, the one I'd come out of, and upon touching it I realized it wasn't locked, but had merely been closed by the wind; so I opened it and hopped in. Unbelievable! How could I have been so stupid? How could it have closed shut, without a spring-lock? Perhaps the hook had been only partially inserted … I had to test it out. So I went back out on the ledge, partially inserted the hook and closed the window from the outside. The hook fell the rest of the way forward and locked the window for good. I was quite satisfied with myself, as my theory had proved correct. I saw a pigeon glaring at me - to say nothing of the ants. All right, I agree, a little more good sense wouldn't have hurt, but I wasn't about to accept criticism from a vagabond pigeon or a band of ants. I decided to go look for an opening, making my way along the ledge all the way around the house, something I'd initially avoided doing in order not to risk being seen by someone on the street or worse, by Petulla. This operation didn't turn out to be overly challenging, except for the points in which the gargoyles hindered my passage. If that weren't enough, my neighbor's rascal of son threw his two cents in as well. As soon as I came in range, he took advantage and let me have it with his peashooter. Finally I reached the back corner of the house where the gutter ran down. If

I were able to use it to let myself down, I could finally get back on the ground. As I prepared for this last stunt, I heard a very familiar voice call to me from down in the street, "My fearless little sweetie pie, what are you doing hanging up there? Have you decided to commit suicide?"

CHAPTER 9

There could be no doubt - it was really her, the one and only Lorelai. Seated atop her Dutch bicycle with her backpack on her shoulders, she was looking me over from top to bottom, her eyes wide in amazement.

As I made my way down the gutter she leaned her bicycle against the wall, put her backpack down and, as soon as I was on the ground, she ran to embrace me.

"Where have you been?" I asked her.

"I was mad at you," she replied. "What kind of an idea was that, leaving me alone with *her*! As soon as you went down to go fix that car, I packed my bag and took off. I've been in the countryside with my friend Theodosia for a few days." Her face darkened as she recalled these things, but then she smiled, kissed me on the nose, and added, "But I'm over it now, I forgive you. I realize you only did it because you're a chivalrous old fool.

I pretended not to have heard. But while Lorelai was using a twig to try to remove a piece of gum that had stuck to the bottom of one of her shoes, she said, "I wanted to ask you a couple of things. Have you gotten rid of that fashion model from outer space yet? And what were you doing up there on the ledge?"

I brought her up to speed. The first part of my story, regarding the prison planet in the far-off Orion galaxy, amazed her to no end, but when she heard the news about Petulla, she her furious.

"How dare that idiot go around dressed up as me!"

"Don't worry," I reassured her. "We'll get everything resolved. Come on, let's put the bike in the garage. We've already run a huge risk of being seen."

After concealing the bicycle in the garage behind the carriage, we reached the library at the top of the tower through a secret passage my great-grandfather had built to escape the ghost of his second wife. I needed time to study the case, so I decided we would camp out right there in the library. I began to read everything I had about spaceships and extraterrestrials. Lorelai assisted me in my research, though at times her choice of sources, such as the books of Star Wars and Star Trek, or my Jeff Hawke and Flash Gordon comics, were slightly off target.

It was very strange to spend all those hours in the library with the real Lorelai and then go down at meal time to find the false version.

To the latter, I'd explained that I was doing

some research on mole tunnels, and she was quite happy not to have me around all day long, though she was amazed at how many sandwiches I was bringing with me each day for snacks.

I read so much I nearly went blind. I couldn't believe there was such a vast literature on the topic of UFOs. I would never have thought, for example, that on Uranus they organized the most important festival of alien music in the entire Milky Way, or that on the planet Derz in the Andromeda galaxy they sold eyeglasses that allowed you to see through walls. By the end I knew so much on the topic that I considered the idea of organizing a series of conferences, for which I would naturally charge admission.

Then, one evening, I finally found the information I was looking for. I read in the eighth number of *UFOs and Martians* magazine that mutants are allergic to radishes. Eating even a single one made them fall into a deep sleep that would last for a hundred years unless Prince Charming etc. etc.

Good, this was it. And it just so happened that the next day it would be my turn to cook. The only thing left to do was to run over to Gunnar's and buy a nice supply of radishes. Lorelai jumped for joy, and not only because she couldn't bear to stay in the library anymore, despite the fact that every evening we climbed to the top of the tower to gaze at the stars.

Usually we sat on the ground to watch the sky and, this way, the little crenellated wall protected us from prying eyes. But that evening, Lorelai was so happy that she started dancing underneath the full moon and thus, passing through the hallway that looked out on the inner courtyard, Petulla saw us.

CHAPTER 10

The following morning the sun rose punctually as it always did, completely unaware that it was thus firing the starting gun on our very own personal Judgment Day. But we mustn't be too amazed at this since, when it's all said and done, the sun, always busy with its explosions and nuclear reactions, has bothered too much about human affairs. Or perhaps it did, who knows? In any case, I went early to Gunnar's and bought up all the radishes I could find. I also purchased some radicchio, tomato, fennel, and onions to prepare a big salad in which the radishes could be camouflaged. As I returned home with the groceries I felt great. Things finally seemed to be going right. After its umpteenth turn, the world was again showing me its best side. Suddenly, however, I felt a slight shiver run down my spine. It was my sixth sense warning me of an imminent change in events. Indeed, Lorelai suddenly leaned out from the top of the tower and started yelling at me, "Watch out, sweetie pie! Watch out, sweetie pie!"

Watch out for what, damn it to hell! If there was one thing I couldn't stand, it was a vague warning. I looked around but didn't see anything anywhere, except a pigeon that looked at me worriedly, as if to say, "You're not thinking about coming back out on the ledge, are you?"

As I looked back up for an explanation from Lorelai, the garage door suddenly shattered into a thousand pieces and that enormous, crab-shaped robot I'd glimpsed while looking in through the windows of the red room came running out on all six of its mechanical legs, stopping in the middle of the street just in front of me. I couldn't help but admire the technical ability with which it had been constructed and, even aesthetically speaking, it wasn't bad at all. Several moments of silence followed; then the large door on the back of the crab slowly opened and out rose a being, visible up to the waist, that combined a fundamentally human shape with an assortment of features taken from the animal world. It had the head of an owl with deer's horns and a rather long, scaly neck attached to a body covered with bristly hair. From its back there sprouted two large bat wings and, in addition to a pair of brawny, green arms, it also had on its front two long thin arms like those the praying mantis uses to grasp the male after copulation and devour him like a ham sandwich. Luckily, I could not see the lower part of the body. That absurd, monstrous creature was obviously Petulla, and she had unleashed her imagination to create something truly awful. If she thought she could shock me with this spectacle, she was right- but not as much as she thought. I had been stunned much more that time, near the Strofades, when I'd found myself face to face with a horde of raging harpies after I'd stolen a pair of their underwear on a stupid bet.

Since to me this silence had gone on long enough, I broke the ice, saying, "So? Do we have to stand here all day just staring at each other? I do have other things to do before nightfall."

"Stupid earthling!" it exclaimed with a shriek that once again made me think of those harpies, "There shall be no more nights for you! Know that, as of this moment, the conquest of your planet has begun. Millions of crabs like this one are on their way from space. I am merely the front line."

Beside the fact that even children know that crabs can't fly, this seemed to be the same old story I'd heard time and time again. How many movies had I seen about invasions of Earth? I would've liked to explain to her that, at the end of all these films, the aliens always took a licking, and that therefore it would have been better off packing up and going home, but something told me this argument wouldn't have been too convincing. So I decided to try the sentimental approach.

"But Petulla," I said with a charming voice, "You like me, you can't deny it. You can't deny that we had something that would have made us both happy. Now look what's become of you, you look like a concoction of zoo concentrate. But I know this isn't you, for I've known a very different you. How can you throw away our happiness, just like that? Have you perhaps forgotten about that evening when we first met in the rain, under that street lamp? You should know that for me, ever since that moment, all other women have ceased to exist."

I heard a moan coming from the top of the tower, but I wasn't about to be distracted, continuing: "Just think, my precious, of what you're giving up. We could get married, have children. Can't you already hear the pitter patter of their little feet as they run around the house, the crash of a jar of jam as it breaks in the pantry because those little rascals were trying to steal it?"

I realized that my words had not been without effect, as a tear was now streaking Petulla's owlish face. I decided to take my performance to the next level: "What do you care about conquering an entire planet if you lose the chance that destiny's given you to be happy? Sure, your superiors will say "nice work," they might even give you a nice medal, but when you're old, sad, and alone, and, hunched over in your rocking chair, you see that dusty medal hanging from a fireplace whose fire has long been extinguished, you'll regret ..."

No further words were necessary. For good reason I had been a famous actor and graced the stages of the world's most important theaters. In an instant, Petulla turned back into the lovely green alien I'd known in the beginning and told me, "Wait for me just one moment," and disappeared inside the crab-robot.

As soon as she was gone, I felt some drops fall on my head and thought it was starting to rain again. I looked up and realized that it wasn't rain, but rather Lorelai softly crying at the top of the tower and repeating over and over with a barely audible voice, "But I thought ... but I thought ..."

I had taken it for granted she would understand that the sugar-coated words I'd spoken to Petulla were false, but I had miscalculated. As so often had in the theater with my moving performances, I had succeeded in completely stunning and capturing my audience, and had now been so convincing that Lorelai had fallen into my trap just as much as Petulla. Talent can't be bought, as they say. I was sorry for this little mix-up but, for the moment, it couldn't be helped; I would explain everything afterwards. Petulla jumped out of the crab as happy as a clam and ran to embrace me.

"Everything has been sorted out," she told me, "I stopped the invasion. I told General Slowpoke there is nothing interesting to be conquered on Earth and handed in my resignation. Now I am all yours."

I heard a lament coming from the tower.

"What was that?" asked Petulla.

"Nothing," I answered, "Maybe a pigeon who's had too much to eat. You know how these pigeons are."

Luckily that was Lorelai's last lament. She finally understood my ploy when she heard me say to her hated rival, "My darling, now we must celebrate. On these occasions, here on Earth we usually eat a radish and, wouldn't you know it, I just happen to have a few kilos of them with me."

A moment later I was the one would have willingly let out a groan when Petulla responded, "I'm sorry. Maybe you did not know, but like all mutants I am allergic to radishes."

CHAPTER 11

So she knew! That piece of information whi-ch I'd found with such great effort in the eighth issue of *UFOs and Martians* magazine and upon which I'd based my entire plan of action now ran the risk of being completely useless! My mind searched frenetically for a new solution and, after a couple of minutes, I'd already found it. That phosphorus-based therapy I'd gone through the previous winter seemed to have had some beneficial effects after all. The idea was quite simple, really. If Petulla wouldn't eat a radish of her own free will, I'd slip her one on the sly. It was no coincidence that one of my ancestors, before being poisoned to dea-th, had been a close friend of Lucrezia Borgia. I began to relax, considering that my plan was simple to put into effect and sure to succeed. The road to victory was once again obstacle-free. I took Petulla's arm with the intention of setting off toward the house, but first I said to her, "It's best you get that giant crab out from the middle of the street."

How could I have forgotten how difficult she

was, how she was always looking for a fight, and how she always had some smart-aleck reply in store for me?

"How dare you tell me what to do!" she promptly shot back. "Remember that, on my planet, the women are the ones in charge! I will remove the spaceship how, when and if I want to."

I didn't want to anger her and thus compromise my plan, so I told her in a conciliatory tone, "But of course, dear ... I didn't mean ..."

"Do not start groveling like a dog now," she continued, "What kind of a man are you? If you want to be with me, you need to change your tone. If you think you can go on leading this debauched life you have had up to now, you have another thing coming! First, you are going to cut off that ridiculous moustache; then, you are going to stop dressing like a dandy; and you are going to start waking up at five o'clock every morning to exercise. The whole house will then have to be refurnished. We will go down to the landfill and get rid of the trash in there now and I will order new furniture in the pure, psycho-cubic style of my planet. And while I go freshen up, you can get to work repairing the garage door."

Having said this, she spun around and set off toward the house. But she never reached the door: for from the first-floor window, Lorelai hit her on the head with the 9th century Ming-Ting-Tong vase she'd just finished gluing back together. I looked up and saw her waving at me from the window with a radiant smile.

"Sweetie pie," she said, "you have no idea how long I've wanted to do that."

I dragged Petulla into the house and Lorelai met me by the stairs. I embraced her and said, "Nice work." Then, I went back down into the street and pushed the crab-robot into the garage so as not to tempt fate any further, since it had been kind enough to ensure that no one had walked by up to that moment.

After all that commotion it was time to relax for a bit, so I took a seat on the orange couch. Lorelai immediately cuddled up next to me and began to purr.

"You know" I told her, "Petulla is nothing like you at all."

"But you still went as soft on her as a cooked pear."

I didn't appreciate being compared to a cooked pear, so I immediately rebutted.

"She cooks very well, you know," I told her.

"It's not too late, my boiled little sweetie pie. If you'd like, I'll wake her up for you and go pack my bags."

"Don't be ridiculous."

After several minutes of silence, Lorelai asked me, "What do we do with her now? Shall we put her down in the crypt with Uncle Mortimer?"

What an idea! Why ever do something so nasty to poor old Uncle Mortimer? Not for a moment did I consider such an absurd sugge-stion; rather, I got to thinking about a solution. After one minute and forty-three seconds I had it - I only needed to verify one thing. I went down to the garage, and it was just as I'd thought - that big crab was the same space-ship that had previously been parked on the street in the shape of a car. Petulla had merely altered its shape. Good, now we needed to hurry since our alien wasn't going to stay knocked out forever, though getting hit on the head with a 9th century Ming-Ting-Tong vase was certainly no laughing matter. I asked Lore-lai to help me and together we brought Petulla down to the garage and got her nice and com-fortable in the driver's seat of the spaceship. Then I leaned in the window to turn the igni-tion key. Since I hadn't de-activated the alarm, Petulla would be teleported onto that same, fa-r-off prison planet where I'd ended up. And they wouldn't let her leave until she became honest and good. I was just congratulating my-self on my truly excellent plan and reaching to turn the key, when all of a sudden Petulla awo-ke and grabbed me by the neck. She was in-stantly transformed into a gorgeous, but fero-cious, green tiger and I immediately turned into the hairy, sharp-toothed monster Grunz. It was an epic struggle with sparks flying every-where, and all in the close confines of the spa-ceship's cabin. It was as if two rabid cats had been shut together inside a can. I was, as usual, about to win when that treacherous mutant pulled the dirty trick of suddenly doubling her own size. She barely fit into the cabin anymore, and I no longer knew where to bite. I think that such a move would've been severely prohibited by intergalactic regulations, if there'd ever been any. For the first time, the monster Grunz was about to bite the dust. Petulla opened her jaws to administer the *coup de grace* when, through the open window, Lorelai threw a radish smack into her wide open jaws. Petulla immediately reassumed her true features and fell into a deep sleep. Since she'd been standing over me in that moment, she literally fell right into my arms and lay down lengthwise on top of me.

Lorelai looked in through the window and commented, "I thought using that radish was a smart move, but judging by the results I'm not so sure."

Having freed myself of that extraterrestrial burden and reassumed my true appearance, I got out of the spaceship and banged my head against the wall to get some relief from my headache. Then I took Lorelai in my arms and kissed her. She was now back to her cheerful self again, and I was sure of it because she immediately started prancing around. We then sent Petulla off to the Orion galaxy with a sign around her neck, saying that if any Prince Charming happened to read this sign, they could kiss her and wake her up.

That evening, after dinner, we were going up to the tower to play the balalaika and dance by the light of the moon, when the doorbell rang. It was Petulla, and when Lorelai saw her reappear, she nearly fainted.

She had come back on the very same evening of her departure. But for her thirty-five years had passed – the length of time it had taken her to redeem herself and become good. Her looks hadn't changed at all, but inside she truly was a different person. To earn our forgiveness, she went as far as to clean the entire house, fix up the garden, and repaint the yellow, blue, and purple bathrooms. Too bad that, as we discovered only later, she was color blind. We had to let her stay with us for another three days to give her time to finish, a situation which made Lorelai lose her appetite and develop the hiccups. When Petulla finally decided to leave, no tears were shed. Indeed, each of us had our good reasons for being happy about it. Lorelai, because Petulla was finally gone; Petulla, since, after thirty-five years, she was finally going home; and me, because if living with Lorelai was fine – great, in fact - living with two women was utter madness. Two was one too many.